# Sometimes Noise is Big

*by the same author*

**A Guide to Sometimes Noise
is Big for Parents and Educators**
*Angela Coelho and Lori Seeley*
*Illustrated by Camille Robertson*
ISBN 978 1 78592 374 6
eISBN 978 1 78450 720 6

# SOMETIMES NOISE IS
# BIG

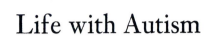

## Life with Autism

Angela Coelho

Illustrated by Camille Robertson

**Jessica Kingsley Publishers**
London and Philadelphia

First published in 2018
by Jessica Kingsley Publishers
73 Collier Street
London N1 9BE, UK
and
400 Market Street, Suite 400
Philadelphia, PA 19106, USA

*www.jkp.com*

**Library of Congress Cataloging in Publication Data**
A CIP catalog record for this book is available from the Library of Congress

**British Library Cataloguing in Publication Data**
A CIP catalogue record for this book is available from the British Library

ISBN 978 1 78592 373 9
eISBN 978 1 78450 719 0

Printed and bound in China

Aidan and Lysia,
thank you for showing me
the world as you see it.

Sometimes when I wake up in the morning, the light is **REALLY LOUD** and it hurts my eyes.

TICK TOCK

Sometimes noise is **REALLY BIG**,

even when it is small for everyone else.

Sometimes I am so excited
that I need to **SCREAM**

and run in circles to let it out.

Sometimes feelings are **SO HUGE**, I feel like they are a **GIANT WAVE**

crashing

down

on

me.

Sometimes my clothes feel **ITCHY**

and **HURT** my skin,

even when they are
fine for other people.

Sometimes my mouth
doesn't like how food **FEELS**,

even if
it **TASTES**
really good.

Sometimes it seems like everything is going ***SO FAST*** around me,

I can't focus on one thing.

Sometimes my world is so **BUSY** and **ALIVE**,

I need to sit on my own and shut it out for a while.

Sometimes I need to put things in **ORDER** in a way

that makes sense to me, even if you can't see it.

Sometimes I see things **DIFFERENTLY** than you,
because I am looking at them from my point of view.

Sometimes I can **REMEMBER** big things that I have only seen once, and sometimes I **FORGET** little things I do every day.

Sometimes I **SEE** the words in my head,
but I can't make them **COME OUT**.

Sometimes I feel like no one **UNDERSTANDS** me,

but then you help me just when I need it the most.

It's time to be in bed.

Sometimes I do ***EXACTLY*** what you ***SAID***,

but not exactly what you ***ASKED***.

Sometimes I feel like I am **DIFFERENT** from everybody else,

but then I find things that are the same too.

Sometimes I work so hard to keep myself **CALM** all day,

just to come home

and let out all my feelings at once.

Sometimes I need to be in a **TIGHT SPACE**.
It helps me feel calm, safe, and relaxed.

Sometimes all the **LIGHT** and **NOISE** around me is too much to handle, so I scream and kick or get quiet and don't move.

Sometimes I **TAP** or **SNAP** my fingers or **ROCK** back and forth.

It's a way to keep myself calm.

Sometimes I want to go and make **FRIENDS**
with other kids,

but I don't always know
what to do and need help.

Sometimes you have to
**SLOWLY SHOW** me how to do
something for me to learn it.
**TELLING** me doesn't always work.

Sometimes I see
a ***DIFFERENT***
way to do

what you are asking me to,
it doesn't mean I'm not listening to you.

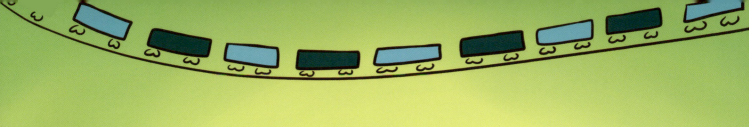

Sometimes I get **SO EXCITED** about something

that it is **ALL** I talk about.

I am just excited about what I like and am trying to **SHARE** it with you.

His writing is hard to read, and he's struggling in gym, too.

Sometimes I wish people would see all the things I can do **WELL**, instead of just what I can't do.

Sometimes I forget to say, "**I LOVE YOU**,"

but I try to show you in my own ways.